DUBLIN
FOLK TALES
FOR CHILDREN

DUBLIN
FOLK TALES
FOR CHILDREN

ÓRLA MC GOVERN

ILLUSTRATED BY GALA TOMASSO

The
History
Press

*This book is dedicated
to Niceol, with love.*

Special thanks to Zita, Deirdre, Gala, Eunice, Pamela,
Tyrone Guthrie Centre, and all the family and friends
who have inspired me with stories and ideas.

First published 2018

The History Press
The Mill, Brimscombe Port
Stroud, Gloucestershire, GL5 2QG
www.thehistorypress.co.uk

© Órla Mc Govern, 2018
Illustrations © Gala Tomasso, 2018

The right of Órla Mc Govern to be identified as the Author
of this work has been asserted in accordance with the
Copyright, Designs and Patents Act 1988.

British Library Cataloguing in Publication Data.
A catalogue record for this book is available from the British Library.

ISBN 978 0 7509 8423 2

Typesetting and origination by The History Press
Printed and bound by CPI Group Ltd

Contents

About Us

Órla Mc Govern is a writer, storyteller and performer. She grew up in Dublin, travelled around the world for a bit, and now lives in Galway on the West Coast of Ireland. She loves making things up – stories, songs, plays, sometimes just dinner! Some of her favourite stories, she says, are the ones that are full of strange sounds and surprises. Just like some of her favourite people!

Gala Tomasso studied Art & Design in England, Fine Art at the Burren College of Art in Clare, and Design in DIT Dublin. Originally from Scotland, she has had her roots in Galway for twenty-five years and currently lives in Connemara.

Introduction

Hello Readers! I hope you enjoy this book. It's a collection of folk tales from Dublin.

Some people wonder what the phrase 'folk tales' means. Well, the way I see it, the clue is right there in the words themselves. Folk tales are tales from folks, simple as that. Some stories might be quite old and passed on down through the years. Others might be new, and more again are a mix of both old and new. Folk tales can be stories inspired by a particular place, a particular person, a particular animal, or even a particular tree!

I'm very fond of trees myself. In fact, there are a couple of tree stories in this book. I often think of tales and stories themselves as being a bit like trees. Over the years they grow and change. Two people might look at the same tree – one in spring, one in winter – and see it very differently, just as two people might tell the same story in very different ways.

Sometimes bits of a story can 'fall away' (a bit like old branches and leaves from a tree). Sometimes, new bits pop up when people invent new parts (a bit like the fresh shoots in spring). Stories are there to be explored and climbed. Some stories may give fruit (another story)! And some may be a bit thorny, or even smelly!

When we hear stories of our history, the roots are often the same, but you are never quite sure in which direction the branches will twist.

This book is called *Dublin Folk Tales for Children,* so the stories in it are all connected to Dublin, and, of course, anyone can enjoy a good story, no matter what age they are.

Dublin City is the place where I was born and where I grew up. The roots of these stories came to me from loads of places: my grandparents; neighbours; friends (thanks everyone); from reading books, and, of course, from my imagination.

There are folk tale books from other towns and countries, too, and the funny thing is, you'll often find two stories that are quite alike, even though they grew from very different places. I wonder why that is? Perhaps it's because stories float about from place to place like little seeds and then take root?

I've been asked to write this book in an 'out loud' storytelling style. What that means is that I've written the words a bit more like you might say them than (usually) write them.

Some of the words may have strange spellings (I bet you can spot them) or 'slang' words, because they are written to sound like a person telling them out loud. There are a few

stories that have sound effects in them too. It can be great fun to read these stories aloud. Try them out on your friends!

You can read the words, and you can also try to see if you can just *remember* the stories, and tell them your own way. You might find a new shoot of leaves popping out of your story tree! Perhaps these stories will inspire you to make your own!

Is there an interesting place or an animal or tree in your area that you would like to make a story about? Is it connected to something from history, or just your imagination? Give it a try. You can write a story, tell a story, or both! Does it sound different when you say it out loud?

Have fun discovering all the different shoots, branches, leaves, fruit, and maybe even a few magical birds' nests that you discover while growing your own stories.

I hope I get to hear one or two!

1

Áine's Spoon

Supposing I was to ask you, right this second, to shout out the name of a river in Dublin. Let's try it! Are you ready? Okay. One, two, three – GO!

Great! So how many of you shouted out 'The River Liffey'? Quite a lot of you, I'd imagine, as to loads of people the Liffey is the best-known river in Dublin.

Did anyone say a different river? Good for you!

Well, did you know that there are about 130 different rivers in Dublin City and County? I didn't until I looked it up some years ago!

In olden days, there were a couple of rivers that were very important for the city. People used them to transport themselves and to

transport goods and animals. But did you know
that in the past, some other rivers were just as
important and well known as the Liffey? One
of these rivers is called the Poddle.

Now, not far away from the banks of the
Poddle, there lived a girl called Áine Ryan.

Áine lived in a house full of music. Her Da played the fiddle and her Ma played the guitar. They played lots of different types of music, but they particularly liked to play Trad (that's short for traditional) Irish music.

Sometimes they'd go and play music with other people in pubs, cafés and halls. When people got together, they called it a 'session'. They'd go to places like The Brazen Head, or Hughes' Pub on the Quays. Sometimes, if it was on a Sunday in the daytime, Áine would go with them to listen to the music. Her Da would get her a juice and some crisps and she'd be delighted with herself.

She loved to listen to all the different instruments playing together. Sometimes someone would sing a song without any instruments, just their voice, and everyone would 'shhhhh' so they could be heard.

Áine's Auntie Mary lent her a bodhrán to practise on. A bodhrán is the name for an Irish drum that you play with a stick called a 'beater'. Some people play it with their hand, or a wooden stick, and some even use the bone of an animal!

Áine was over the moon and wanted to play the bodhrán right away at a session, but her Da said she had to practise at home for a while before she could play it 'properly'. Her Da sometimes rolled his eyes at bodhrán players at sessions, and her Ma would elbow him and whisper, 'Stop it, John,' and throw him a smile.

Áine's Da thought people should learn to play the bodhrán well before playing in sessions, because it was a very loud instrument!

Sometimes the musicians would visit Áine's house to play. She loved that, as her Ma would bake buns for the visitors and Áine would be delighted with all the music in the house. She had a great life, and wouldn't change a thing.

Well, maybe one thing.

The one 'thing' Áine would have changed was the presence of a boy who went to her school. His name was James Kavanagh. Now, if your name is James Kavanagh, don't worry. It's not you I mean. Probably.

If you looked up 'nasty' in a dictionary, there was a picture of (this particular) James Kavanagh looking back at you (well not really, dictionaries don't usually have pictures, and I'm just saying that to make the point that this James Kavanagh was NAAAAAASTY). He used to love being a bully and playing mean jokes on people.

He would put thumb tacks on people's chairs before they sat down (ouch)! He would write mean notes on pieces of paper and stick them on people's backs (mean)! But the thing that Áine hated most of all was the 'joke' James would play on people at lunchtime. Well, do you know what, it wasn't even a joke at all, because jokes are meant to be funny.

This was not funny.

If you had a nice bar of chocolate at lunch, James would grab it, lick it, rub it in his armpit (ewwwww!) and give it back to you. Of course at this point you wouldn't want to eat it, because James had licked it and armpitted it (more ewwwww), so you would generally have to throw it in the bin.

Áine hated this.

Then one day, things got even worse. James not only performed his antics with food at lunchtime, but with other things too.

Things like people's pens, their rubbers, and stuff from their pencil cases. And he even found new ways to be disgusting. Sometimes after he had licked the thing, or armpitted it, he would stick it up his nose or in his ear and twist it (even more ewwww)!

And sometimes he would do all of those things together. James really was a pest.

But at the weekends things were different for Áine, at the weekends she was delighted, as she didn't have to think about James Kavanagh and his 'jokes' for even one second. She didn't live near him and she was very happy about that fact.

One Saturday, a lovely day with the sun shining, Áine decided to go for a walk near her house, along the bank of the Poddle.

She noticed there were workers out. They were 'dredging', or cleaning, the river, and there were big piles of clay from the riverbed on the banks. Some of them were a bit stinky as they had rotten weeds in them. Of course, dogs love stinky stuff, and Áine laughed to herself when she saw a dog digging and rolling around in one of the stinky piles. The dog's owner wasn't happy!

'Come out, come out of that, Max!' said the lady. 'Bad dog, oh you smelly dog!'

Of course Max was delighted with himself and trotted off, happy and stinky, behind his annoyed owner.

Now, just as Áine passed by the pile of earth where Max was digging, she thought she spotted something shiny in the weeds.

She walked over. Pheewww! It was stinky. She picked up the tiny thing that she had seen sparkling. What was it? Hmmm.

Well, at first she thought it was a pin or a nail, but when she brushed off the dirt and looked at it more closely, do you know what? It looked like a tiny spoon! Yes, a spoon! Fancy that.

Áine headed home and put the spoon under the tap in the kitchen to wash the rest of the dirt off it. It was a gorgeous little thing. It appeared to be made from silver, and had an

unusual shape, with lovely little designs in the middle.

Definitely a spoon!

Who would have such a tiny spoon, though, and what would they use – WAIT! She knew what it was! It was a FAIRY spoon! Sure it was so tiny, who else could be able to use it? Not only that, but she thought it must be a musical fairy spoon.

Now I should explain, in case you don't know, that in Irish music, people often play an instrument called 'the spoons'.

You can buy a ready-made set of 'spoons' but sometimes, people used to use actual food spoons to play music. They were usually big soup spoons. In the olden days, they even used more bones!

To play them, you would get two big spoons and hold them close together with a finger holding a gap in the middle of them, and you would bang them on your lap, or your other hand, or if you were feeling adventurous, your own head or arm or even someone else's arm!

'Clack, clicky-clack, clicky-clicky-clack, clicky-clicky-clack', they'd go. They're fun to play, you should try it yourself!

Anyway, Áine was convinced that this teeny tiny spoon that she'd found was half of a fairy set of spoons.

Instead of running out and telling her friends or her family, though, Áine decided to keep her new treasure a secret, just for a little while anyway. It made her feel special.

That night she put the fairy spoon under her pillow for safekeeping, and fell asleep.

A dream descended on her, and music filled the air. There she was in the land of Fairy. She was invited to sit in at a fairy session with her new bodhrán. There were six fairy fiddlers, and six fairy flute players, and they were all brilliant!

Beside her, sitting on a stool, was the original owner of 'her' spoon (the fairy spoon player). He was brilliant too, a great musician, and he played his tiny spoons. 'Clack, clicky-clack, clicky-clicky-clack, clicky-clicky-clack', he played.

She picked up the bodhrán and found that she was brilliant at playing it too! 'Dum-tikka-tikka-dum-tikka-tikka-dum-tikka-tikka-dum!'

When Áine woke up from her dream, she was in a great mood altogether. She took her fairy spoon from under her pillow, tucked it into her pencil case and headed off to school. She wasn't going to let it out of her sight!

She was in such a great mood that she nearly forgot all about James Kavanagh and his antics. But when lunchtime rolled around she remembered them very quickly.

First James grabbed poor Mary Kelly's Mars Bar and gave it the armpit treatment. He looked across the room to Áine and gave an awful laugh.

'Lucky I've finished my lunch,' Áine thought. There was nothing for James to 'armpit'. But she was wrong. Just as lunch was finishing, didn't James sneak up and grab Áine's pencil case from the top of her bag.

'Anything interesting for me in here today?' jeered James. 'Give it back, you bully!' Áine said, trying to grab it from him – but he held it high in the air.

'Oh what have we here?' said James, pulling out Áine's spoon from the bottom of the pencil case. 'What's this? Some kind of girrrrrrrrrly jewellery yoke?'

'Don't touch that!' she shouted, but it was too late.

First James licked the top of the spoon, and then he put the whole spoon in his mouth and pretended to swallow it. Then he opened his mouth, and stuck his tongue out to show the spoon was still there on his tongue (ewww)! Then – then what did he do?

Didn't he put the spoon up his nose, and started twirrrrrrling it around, as if he was making a 'snotty candy floss'. Ewwww!

'Oh I forgot a bit!' said James. 'The old armpit!'

He was JUST about to stick it under his smelly armpit, when he felt a hand grab him on the shoulder.

'Where did you get that, James Kavanagh?' boomed a voice. It was the school principal, Mr Kelly.

Everyone liked Mr Kelly but they were just a little bit afraid of him when he used his 'big' voice, because his 'big' voice usually meant someone was in trouble.

Of course, James immediately tried to put the blame on Áine.

'It's not mine sir, it's hers,' he said, pointing to Áine. 'She dropped it so she did, and I was just picking it up!'

Mr Kelly took out a hanky from his pocket and used it to pick the fairy spoon from James's hand.

Áine watched as Mr Kelly carefully folded the handkerchief around the snotty, armpitty, licky spoon and put it in his own pocket. Oh no!

'Both of you, up to my office ... NOW!' said Mr Kelly, in a VERY big and boomy voice.

Well, off went James and Áine to the office to wait outside, throwing each other dirty looks while they sat. When Mr Kelly was ready for them, in they went and sat down in front him. He was sitting behind his big desk and looked

very serious. He had a big stack of books piled up in front of him.

He fixed his eyes on James first. 'Mr Kavanagh, are you sure this doesn't belong to you?' He held up the fairy spoon in his hanky.

'N ... N ... No,' spluttered James. 'It belongs to Áine Ryan, sir.'

Áine could feel herself sinking deeper into her chair.

'Well, Áine,' said Mr Kelly, 'is this true?'

'Yes sir,' she said, honestly.

'And where did you get it?'

'I found it, sir.'

'Where exactly did you find it?'

Áine told Mr Kelly the whole story about walking on the bank of the Poddle, and the stinky piles of dirt from the bottom of the river, and Max the dog, and finding the fairy spoon.

'What did you call it?' said Mr Kelly.

'Emm ... a fairy spoon?'

Mr Kelly smiled, and almost laughed! Then he composed himself and tried to look serious.

'Look at this, children,' he said, and he opened a book and pointed at a big drawing on one of the pages. It was a drawing of the fairy spoon! Well, not exactly. The design on the middle was a little bit different, but they looked really alike.

'This,' said Mr Kelly, 'is a Viking spoon.'

Áine and James looked at each other, a bit confused.

'But sir, I thought the Vikings were very tall people, and sure these two spoons are tiny,' said Áine.

'Ah yes,' said Mr Kelly, holding up the spoon. 'It *is* tiny because it is a Viking EAR spoon.'

'Wha?' said James.

Mr Kelly explained how the Vikings wore these spoons around their necks on a silver chain like a piece of jewellery. Then they would take the spoon, and put it into their ears and use it to scoop out their ear wax (ewww)! A bit like a cotton bud.

Áine looked around at James. He looked a bit green in the face.

'Are you all right, James?' said Mr Kelly, but James shook his head.

Áine realised why James was turning green. He was thinking of where that ear spoon had come from – that big pile of stinky muck from the bottom of the river. He was thinking of where it had been before that – in some big Viking's ear hole full of wax, and he was thinking of where it had been a half an hour ago – in his own ear, his nose, in his mouth ... ewwwwwwwwwww!

Áine couldn't help it; she had a big grin on her face.

Mr Kelly explained how the Vikings had come to Dublin from Scandinavia over a thousand years ago. Ages!

They had settled along the shores of the River Poddle, right near where Áine was walking. When the council workers dug up the mud at the bottom of the river, up came the ear spoon too. It must have been lying there undiscovered for a whole thousand(ish) years.

Now Mr Kelly told Áine that she'd have to hand in her spoon to the people at the National Museum. She was a bit sad at this, but Mr Kelly told her they would take good care of it, and they would put it on display so loads of people could come and see it. That part made her feel a bit better.

But do you know what else? A couple of weeks later, didn't Áine get a letter in the post from the people in the museum. They sent her a very nice thank-you and a reward for turning in the spoon to them. A cheque for three hundred euros!

Well, with that reward money Áine bought herself a brand new bodhrán to play at the session (and promised her Da she would practise loads first).

And do you know what else? Ever since that day James Kavanagh stopped licking people's lunch and stuff and putting it in his armpit. He even started being nicer to people, and that was the biggest reward that Áine could ever hope for!

2

The Two Trees

The Townland of Ballinascorey is situated in County Dublin, right at the edge, where Dublin meets Wicklow. If you were to take a walk there and go up to the top of a certain hill, you would come across an old stone circle. Now nobody is quite sure exactly how long it has been there, but it has definitely been there for a long time!

If you walked up to the circle, one thing you would notice is that there are two trees growing beside it. These are very tall trees, and most likely very old too. It's a little unusual to see two old trees like this on their own, but if you ask someone in the area about them they will probably tell you this story ...

A number of years ago, a farmer who worked the land nearby wanted to cut down the trees and clear a field for cattle.

Now, two old people in the village heard about this and the two of them called at his house and asked him not to do it.

'Those are fairy trees.' one said. 'They have been there as long as we can remember. It would be very bad luck to cut down a fairy tree, never mind two!'

'I don't have a good feeling about it,' said the other.

Instead of agreeing with them, the farmer laughed at them and told them to be on their way.

'Fairy trees,' he thought, 'Bad luck – humph! What an absolute load of codswallop! Sure aren't they only old stories? Fairy trees indeed!'

The next day he set off out through the gate of his farm in his tractor, with his saws on the back, and headed off to cut down the two trees. From the kitchen window, looking out, his wife watched him leave, and she shook her head. Sure didn't she have a bad feeling about it too!

As he drove up the boreen towards the hill, he passed his two sons working in the field. One waved, but the other just shook his head and kept digging. Because, do you know what, he didn't have a good feeling either.

At this point, maybe I should tell you a bit about fairy trees in Ireland, because we have quite a lot of them! They are said to be sacred places where the fairies gather, and sometimes even make their homes. They are often just one sort of tree, like the blackthorn, but to be honest they can be any type of tree, and you can find them all over the country.

Down through the years, people have had a lot of respect for the fairy folk in Ireland, and to chop down a tree was seen as most disrespectful. Sure you can understand that! Imagine someone came and chopped down your house, you wouldn't be very happy would you? Especially if you'd lived in it for a thousand years!

Anyway, back to the farmer. So there he was, driving uphill to the trees at the top of the hill. He was nearly there. The stone circle was in his sights, when didn't the strangest thing happen.

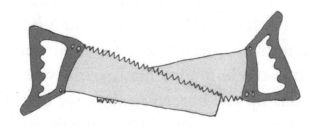

The ground before him began to swell and sway, as if it was a wave on the sea! Now, he thought for a second that his wheel had gone down into a hidden ditch, but of course he knew this was a smooth enough boreen, and he'd been up it countless times, and never before had seen this.

Next thing didn't the ground swell up like a wave big enough to go surfing on! The saws came flying off the back, the tractor was thrown up into the air and the farmer himself was thrown up even higher.

He landed in a crumpled heap on the side of the ditch, and the big wheel of his tractor came crashing down right beside him. A few more inches and it would have landed on him and squished him flat as a pancake!

The farmer cried out in pain. His leg was twisted where he landed on it, and he was certain that it was broken. When the farmer didn't come home for his tea, his wife sent his sons up the boreen to look for him. Of course, when they found him lying there, they rushed him off to the hospital to get his leg seen to.

As they took him down the hill the farmer looked back to where he had fallen. The ground was as flat as it always was – no sign of any disturbance. All he could see was the two trees looking down at him from the top of the hill.

Well, a few days later didn't his wife and his two sons come in to visit him in the hospital. His leg was strung up in a big cast, and the doctors said he wouldn't be able to do much farm work for a couple of months. This meant that his sons would have to take on extra, so they began making a list of things to do.

'The cows ... grand, the hay, fix the shed,' said one son as he went through the list of jobs that he needed to take on.

'And what about those two trees – you never got to cut them, Da?'

The mother and the younger son looked at each other and exchanged a frown.

'Sure I'll make a start on them tomorrow, so

I will,' said the older son, and he stood up to leave.

'Wait!' said the farmer, sitting up a little too suddenly in his bed and wincing from the pain in his leg. 'I think we'll just leave those two big trees where they are for a while.'

The farmer's wife and the younger son exchanged another look.

'Really, Da?' said the older son.

The farmer mumbled something about the trees providing shade on the side of the hill and stopping the soil from shifting, but didn't look his son in the eye as he spoke.

'Ok,' said the older son. 'Now it's nothing to do with all them stories about fa –'

He was just about to say the word 'fairies' when his mother butted in.

'Well, that's enough chatter for today. You rest up now, husband, we'll tend to the farm and we'll be in to see you tomorrow.'

The farmer's wife had seen the flicker of fear on her husband's face. She knew he was afraid that if his sons drove up the hill to try to chop the trees down, that something bad would happen to them, and this time maybe worse than a broken leg! She also knew that he couldn't really let on to his sons that this was the reason, seeing as he had been mocking all the stories before.

'Never mind,' she thought to herself. 'It's better this way. Now my husband won't be ashamed of his fear, my sons will stay safe, and most of all, the two trees will stay where they are meant to be.'

The farmer's wife kissed her husband goodbye, and walked out. As she did, she gave a look to her younger son, and they smiled at each other without saying anything. They both knew that these were indeed fairy trees, and they both wanted them to stay right where they were!

Now was it just some sort of landslide that caused the tractor to tip that day and for the farmer to break his leg? Who knows for sure, but I'll tell you one thing, if you walk up to the top of that hill, to this very day, you will still see those two trees, standing watch over the ancient stone circle.

3

Mister Shh Shh

In Ringsend, on the Southside of Dublin, there used to be a big factory called the Glass Bottle Factory. It was right on the waterfront and it stood really tall up against the skyline. It was near the edge of the water, and the land beside it had lots of hills and dunes to play on. Sometimes things would wash up from the sea nearby – there'd often be bits of rubbish and stuff that people had thrown away (though it's not very nice to throw rubbish into the sea).

Many ships had come and gone from Ringsend and Irishtown over the years. Even that scoundrel Oliver Cromwell had landed his fleet there, so sometimes you could find old stuff like old coins, clay pipes, parts of ships, and other exciting treasures if you looked carefully.

Bits of glass would toss around in the water for years and years. The waves and the sand would wear down the sharp edges, and the bits of glass would be washed up on the shore. These bits came in all sorts of colours, and they looked like beautiful jewels dotted in blobs on the beach. You could pick them up, and they felt lovely in your hands.

They weren't sharp at all except the odd time when a new piece of glass washed up. You had to be careful! That's why people's Mams or Dads weren't too happy when their kids went picking up every little thing that washed up.

'Be careful!', they would say.

But unusually, on this particular beach, there weren't that many sharp ones at all. It was as if someone had gone out and picked them all up and tidied them away. Maybe the people from the glass factory did it?

If you found a lemonade bottle, or two or three, and they weren't broken, you could take them up to the corner shop and swap them for penny sweets! You had to keep a good eye out for them though, as everyone knew this and was on the lookout.

It was a great place to look for treasure, and also a great place to walk and get some air.

Many people walked their dogs around there too. One such person was a character that the local kids called Mr Shh Shh.

Now, different kids would tell you stories about how Mr Shh Shh got his name. It was most likely a nickname you see, as the name Shh Shh would be very unusual as a real last name in Ireland. I've never heard it, anyway.

Some said he got the name because he never spoke at all. To anyone. In fact, he had a little Jack Russell dog, and no one had ever heard it bark either. In fact, no one knew the dog's name, so it too got a nickname: Barko (which was a bit silly of course, because Barko never barked).

Now, other people said that Mr Shh Shh got his nickname because of the sound that his coat made when he walked. Mr Shh Shh wore a very long black leather coat, no matter what the weather, and when he walked the coat would go 'shh–shh'.

But most kids knew the real reason why Mr Shh Shh got his nickname. Often, when kids were playing down by the bottle factory, they would see Mr Shh Shh out walking with Barko. He would bend down, pick something up from the beach, and put it in his pocket. He must have been looking for treasure too. On manys the day Mr Shh Shh would stop, look up and close his eyes, as if he was listening out for something. Or someone.

Of course, this made the kids curious. They would run over, and shout at Mr Shh Shh.

'What are you listening to, Mister?'

'What are you doing, Mister?'

'Can Barko come play with us, Mister?'

Mr Shh Shh would open his eyes, as if someone had disturbed him, and say, 'Shh! Shh!'

The kids would laugh, and keep talking to him.

'Can Barko play with us, Mister? Please, Mister?'

Mr Shh Shh would often shake his head and let Barko off his leash to run off with the kids to play (Barko loved it!). And Mr Shh Shh would be left standing on the hill, his eyes closed again. Sometimes he'd stand like that for ages.

Now, one month a new kid came to town. His name was Séamus. He lived in Cork, but he was spending the summer in Dublin with his cousins, as his Mam was sick and needed to rest a bit. Séamus liked his new city and his new friends, and loved to go hunting for treasure down by the Glass Bottle Factory with them.

He saw Mr Shh Shh and asked his cousins who he was. They told him the story, and how he was a bit of a mystery man and how he never spoke. Séamus thought this was very strange.

'Has no one asked him why he stands there with his eyes closed?' he asked.

The kids looked around at each other, with puzzled looks on their faces. No, nobody had.

The next day when the kids saw Mr Shh Shh walking down again, they did their usual, 'Mister, can we play with Barko, please?'

Again, Mr Shh Shh opened his eyes, said with a frown 'Shh, Shh', and let Barko off his leash. Most of the kids ran off to play with the little dog, but Séamus stayed behind.

'What are you listening to, Mister?' said Séamus.

Now Mr Shh Shh was just about to say 'Shh, Shh' Séamus, when he opened his eyes, and saw that Séamus was not teasing him, but genuinely asking a question. Séamus noticed that Mr Shh Shh seemed to have sad eyes, but he looked at Séamus and gave a smile.

It was a tiny smile but it was the first one that Séamus had seen him do. But Mr Shh Shh never answered the question. Instead, he clapped his hands, and sure enough, Barko came running over. Mr Shh Shh put Barko on his leash and started to walk off.

Now Séamus was even more curious than ever; he ran and got his two cousins Aoife and Eoin, and told them of his plan.

'We're going to follow him, come on!'

'Who?' said Aoife.

'Mr Shh Shh – hurry!'

They stayed close, but far enough back so he wouldn't notice them. They followed him at a good distance, down past the grass, and over to where the old warehouses were, down by the factory.

'I think he works as a caretaker,' said Eoin. 'Maybe he's just going to work?'

'It's a Sunday,' said Séamus. 'I think he's up to something!'

The three cousins watched from a distance as Mr Shh Shh made his way down the path past big hedges to a gateway. He pulled out a big bunch of keys, opened the padlock of the gate, and walked in.

'He's left it open!' said Aoife.

The kids followed him in through the gate, being very careful not to be seen.

Around the back of the big hedge was a very large warehouse. It must have been an old one that was used to keep things in years ago. It had huge windows up the side.

Mr Shh Shh took another key and opened the door with it. Very slowly, the kids walked up to the door. They could hear Mr Shh Shh moving around, but they could tell he was down the far end of the big warehouse.

'Now's our chance,' said Séamus. 'Come on!'

They snuck inside the door quickly and quietly, and hid behind a barrel. It was very dark. They could just about make out the shape of Mr Shh Shh over at the other side of the warehouse. Suddenly he turned and walked back towards where they were hiding!

Had he spotted them?

No. He noticed the door was open, and had walked over to bolt it shut. They were still behind the barrel. He hadn't spotted them, but now they were trapped inside! Even if they could pull open that big bolt, he would hear them open it!

They watched, and could just about make out as Mr Shh Shh walked over with Barko to a huge window. He pulled a rope down, and the cloth over the huge window fell to the ground and the light rushed in. Aoife, Eoin and Séamus were shocked at what they saw in front of them!

High in the ceiling of the warehouse were three wooden beams, and hanging from them were hundreds and hundreds of pieces of string. They were different lengths, and at the end of each one was a knot with a piece of glass tied to it! Some pieces of glass were sharp and jagged, others were full bottles, and in all different colours and sizes – all dangling in the air from the strings.

Mr Shh Shh walked over to the corner of the warehouse and pulled out what looked like two long thin sticks. And then didn't he do the strangest thing – he began to 'ching ching' the sticks against the glass.

It was a gorgeous sound, like tiny bells, and piano keys, and little voices singing!

As he played the pieces of glass with the sticks, the glass moved around, and the reflection of the light through each one made designs of different colours and shapes dance on the wall and the floor. There was so much blue and green, it looked like Mr Shh Shh was playing the sea itself!

Eoin let out a loud gasp when he saw this. Mr Shh Shh stopped playing and turned suddenly.

'Is there someone there?', he shouted.

The kids covered their mouths and ducked down more, so they wouldn't be seen. But next thing didn't Barko run right over to where they were hiding. Sure wasn't he only delighted to see his playmates? Mr Shh Shh could see them!

'What are you doing here, children?' This was the first time they had heard Mr Shh Shh speak this much. Ever!

He had an accent that was not from Dublin, not from Ireland, but somewhere else. The children looked at the two sticks in his hand.

'Don't hit us, Mister!' cried Eoin, 'We didn't mean any harm!'

'Hit you? Oh no,' said Mr Shh Shh. 'Oh dear children, no! Did ... did you hear the music?'

The three of them nodded cautiously.

'Did you like it?'

They nodded again, this time a bit more.

'Would you like me to play some more?'

The three cousins exchanged a quick look. Their nervousness was won over by their curiosity, so they nodded a third time!

'Very well,' he said, 'But, as my first audience, you must take the front row seats.'

He threw some sacks on the ground for them to sit on. The kids didn't move at first.

'Please' he said, 'Please be my guests.'

They looked at each other for and then slowly they walked over, lead by Séamus. Barko sat beside him, and Mr Shh Shh resumed playing; the dancing colours and the sounds filled the old warehouse with a magic that's even hard to imagine.

When Mr Shh Shh stopped playing the bottles he turned around. The kids could see that he was smiling, but he had a little bits of tears in his eyes too. Séamus felt a little bit of tears in his own eyes, but he wasn't exactly sure why.

Mr Shh Shh came over and sat down with the kids on the floor, and began to talk to them.

'Thank you for listening to me,' he said. 'You have been my first ever audience.'

They asked him loads of questions, and he answered them as best he could. He told him that his name was Karl. He said he knew that they called him Mr Shh Shh, but he didn't mind.

Karl told them the story of how he had to run away from his own country because it was at war. He pulled out a paper bag of bull's eye

sweets to share, and told them many stories from his life. This was the most Karl had spoken to any person in years!

He said when he came to Ireland he had to leave left everything behind. He was very lonely, but as we know, he didn't like to talk very much.

One day, a few weeks after he arrived, he was down walking by the canal, when didn't he spot a sack on the ground. It was moving! He walked over, opened it and there inside was a little puppy. The poor puppy was barely alive, and had a terrible cold from being outside in the damp. Karl took it home and looked after it. The puppy grew stronger every day and was full of beans but he was never able to bark.

'I called him Sack,' he told the kids, 'because I found him in a sack.'

'We call him Barko,' piped up Aoife.

'I know,' said Karl. 'And that's a much better name. I think he likes it better too, so that's going to be his official name from now on. Barko!'

Barko jumped up when he heard his name being mentioned, and gave Karl a big lick on the face. Everyone laughed.

Karl told more of his stories to the kids and they listened. Karl had lost his wife Elena in the big war. When Karl and Elena had first met, he had gone to see her play the piano in a concert hall. Elena was a wonderful musician, and wrote lots of beautiful music over the years when they were first married.

When Karl came to Ireland during the war, he had to leave all his things behind, including all the books and sheets of music that his wife had written. He had none of Elena's music with him now. The only thing he had were his memories.

Karl told the kids that one day, a few months after arriving in Dublin, he had been out walking on the beach, and he heard the sound of a bottle clinking up against a rock. Then he heard another sound, and another and another, and it reminded him so much of the music that Elena used to play on her piano.

Elena's favourite place to write music had always been by the sea. She composed many songs and pieces of music while watching the waves back in her own country.

Karl believed that maybe the sea itself had captured a little bit of Elena's music and held on to it, like a memory. It had carried her music across the sea to Ireland for him to hear!

He had the idea that he would collect all the bits of glass that washed up. Perhaps the sea had trapped a little bit of Elena's music in each piece of glass. Every day he would take the bottles back to the warehouse, tie them up on a string, hanging from the beam. He would play them with a stick, each one with a different sound, and listen to the notes they made. They reminded him of Elena.

It was getting on for teatime, and time for the kids to go. Karl said goodbye to his guests, and gave each of them a bottle he had collected. Aoife and Eoin turned it in to the corner shop for sweets, but Séamus decided he would keep it as a present for his Mam, when he went home to Cork the next month.

And do you know what, when he gave it to his Mam, she loved it. She put it up on the mantelpiece where it could catch the light from the window. She loved the way the blue colour danced around the room, a bit like the sea.

'It cheers me up,' she'd say to Séamus and she'd smile.

Now loads of those kids who were around in the time of Mr Shh Shh (who we now know was called Karl), are all grown up. Some of them even have kids and grandkids of their own. Some have moved away to other places but a few of them still live down by Irishtown and Ringsend.

Some of them still go out walking still with their own dogs, down near where the Glass Bottle Factory used to be. If you're down by there yourself, out for a walk, you might see a person or two or three standing with their eyes closed, facing out to the sea. You might say hello to them, and of course they might say hello back.

But if one of them turns around to you and goes, 'Shh, Shh', please don't be offended. They might just be taking a break to listen to the music that's captured by the sea.

4

The Little Flower

There was once a great chieftain called the O'Brinn. He was from Wicklow but lived in a town to the west over in Dublin called Chapelizod.

The O'Brinn was a powerful man, but sometimes power and wealth attracts jealousy from others. The O'Brinn lived with his wife and their daughter, Eibhleen. Everyone in the village loved Eibhleen, and often you'd hear them say what a smart and beautiful girl she was. She loved her Mam and Dad very much. Her parents liked to call Eibhleen their 'little flower' as she was so precious to both of them.

To the east of where they lived was an area called Castleknock. You'd probably guess it from the name, but Castleknock had a castle in it.

In that castle lived a man called Hugh Tyrrell. He was first Baron of Castleknock. He was a good man, easy to get along with, and quite fair as a ruler. One day, he was called away from the castle to attend an important meeting. He had to travel far for this meeting and he ended up being away from home for much longer than he thought.

Now, while he was away, didn't his brother Roger Tyrrell jump at the chance to take over the castle! Roger was very different from his brother Hugh. In fact Roger was cruel and mean and liked to be horrible to people. He took what he wanted, whenever he wanted and without asking. He was generally all-around nasty!

One summer's evening, he decided he would take his men and go on a raid – just for fun! He rode his horses over to Chapelizod, and when night fell, didn't himself and his men sneak in, kidnap Eibhleen O'Brinn, and take her back to Castleknock Castle with them!

Eibhleen was fighting with him all the way back, but it was no use, there were too many men guarding her, and she couldn't escape no matter how hard she tried.

Back at Castleknock Castle, Roger locked Eibhleen in a tower, and told her he would be back for her the next morning, and then she would have to marry him!

Now the last thing Eibhleen wanted to do was to marry someone like nasty old Roger. Inside the tower, she looked around, searching for a way out. But it was no use, there was no means to escape. The windows were too small and too high to fit a whole person through them. You could only just about fit one arm through the gap in the stone. There was only one door, and it was locked securely. Roger Tyrrell had even put a guard at the bottom of the winding stair to make sure any prisoners stayed put.

Eibhleen was well and truly trapped!

All day Eibhleen sat in the tower, thinking about what would happen to her once she was married to Roger. She would no longer be free, she would have to live wherever nasty Roger her husband-to-be commanded (for that was the way at the time)! And she would generally be miserable all round.

As the night went on, Eibhleen heard voices at the bottom of the stairs. It was the guards. She heard them talking about the wedding that would happen in the morning, and how they were ordered to take her from the tower directly to Roger at sunrise. They were laughing away to themselves at the whole idea of her being married off to Roger Tyrrell. There was no escaping it!

The minutes ticked into hours and poor Eibhleen was very sad.

Then, just as the sun was beginning to rise, Eibhleen heard a whisper from outside the tiny window. 'Eibhleen,' said the voice. 'It is our turn now to help you!'

There, outside below, growing against the castle wall, was a beautiful cluster of white flowers – that was where the voice was coming from!

'Listen carefully,' said the flowers. 'We can help you escape, but it will come with a price.'

'I will pay any price,' said Eibhleen, 'once I am free from this place and can live in peace once more with my family.'

'Very well,' whispered the flowers. 'The price to pay is that you must shed your human form. Listen carefully and do exactly as we bid you, and you shall be free once more.'

Eibhleen listened to the instructions, and was a little frightened at the thought, but knew it was her only hope.

She had a vision of her Mam and Dad talking to her, smiling at her, calling her their 'little flower'.

Eibhleen reached down and unfastened the brooch from her dress. It was her favourite piece of jewellery; one her mother had given her on her seventeenth birthday. It was a cluster of rubies set in gold, and it looked just like a beautiful bouquet of red flowers.

She walked over to the window. As she leaned in enough she could just about see the

ground below where there were hundreds of white flowers growing beside the castle wall.

'Let us help you ...' they whispered.

Eibhleen could hear the footsteps of the guards on the stairs – it was time to put the plan in action!

She quickly made a wish, took the pin of her brooch, and with it she pricked her finger. Ouch! She watched as a tiny red bump appeared. Eibhleen reached her arm through the narrow window and let it hang down the side of the castle wall.

She could hear the guards fumbling for their keys outside the door!

Drip!

A tiny drop of blood fell from her fingertip and landed on to the white flowers below.

The guards outside had put the key in the lock!

Drip!

A second drop fell from her finger.

The key turned in the lock.

'Oh please hurry,' thought Eibhleen, and she squeezed her finger and –

Drip!

A third drop fell onto the white flowers below just as the door swung open and in marched the guards.

But inside there was no Eibhleen to be found!

There was no one to marry the evil Roger that day. All they found was a ruby and gold brooch lying on the ground, and on its pin was a tiny drop of blood.

Tyrrell's men searched high and low but there was no trace of their captive, and nobody could explain how she got away. As they left the tower, they walked past a single cluster of beautiful red flowers, growing there amid the white ones.

''Tis a pity the maiden has escaped,' said one guard. 'What fine flowers they would have been for a wedding bouquet …'

Now Eibhleen's father, The O'Brinn, had also been away for some nights, and when he returned and heard of his daughter's capture, he was full of anger and sadness. The next night, he and his army attacked Castleknock Castle and defeated Roger Tyrrell and his men, killing them all as the clock struck midnight.

Alas, his beloved daughter was gone without a trace, or so he thought.

As he was leaving to go home to Chapelizod, The O'Brinn noticed the beautiful patch of red flowers growing by the castle wall. They reminded him of his daughter, and he walked over to them.

No sooner had he kneeled down to look at the red blooms, didn't they whisper to him, 'Oh Father dear, I am so glad to see you!'

The chieftain rubbed a tear from his eye as he realised that this was no ordinary gift of nature.

This was indeed his daughter. In order to escape her captors she had shed her human form and had taken the form of a flower!

He took out his pouch and gently dug up the flowers and took them back to his people. He planted Eibhleen in pride of place, where she could live in peace with her clan. In winter she would sleep in the earth, but each spring she would always return in full bloom. She would whisper the secrets of the earth to her beloved family, and they would water and nurture her, their Eibhleen; their own little flower.

Each year, even to this day, there blooms a bunch of beautiful red flowers, growing free and sparkling in the air with the brightness of a thousand rubies!

5

The Dark Hole

If you like hearing Irish stories, you'll probably hear trees mentioned in them a fair bit. Even in this book perhaps! The reason for this is that trees (and the magic that surrounds them) play an important part in the old stories of our lands.

In the olden days of Ireland, it was even written into the law itself that if you felled certain trees without permission, you would be punished. Some trees were considered so important, that the punishment for chopping one down could even be death!

Now if a tree is uprooted suddenly, be it a fairy tree or even a 'regular' tree, it will of course leave a big hole in the ground. Physically, this hole is where the tree itself grew, where the trunk sat, and where the roots spread down into the earth. But there is also something else at play. In some cases, left behind was the magical space that the tree once occupied – a dark hole.

If this dark hole was not properly managed, and the tree had been taken unfairly, it could attract all sorts of creatures and spirits who would make the dark hole their own. Sometimes they could use it to serve their wishes and even take revenge on mortals.

In Dublin, on the north bank of the River Liffey, is a place known as the King's Inns. It is Ireland's oldest law school. It is built on a very old piece of land, and on this land was one of the dark holes that I mention.

A fairy tree was uprooted on this land in ancient times, and a dark hole was left behind. It wasn't long before the dark hole attracted a new resident – a dark, wild and hungry spirit!

Now, people did their best to keep the dark spirit at bay, but it was very powerful. Every fifty years or so, the ground would rumble with the horrible humming of the creature, as it would seek to feed on human flesh!

It is said that the creature would emit a sound from deep in the dark hole; a sound that would hypnotise any young man who happened to be passing. Within a week, the young man would find a young woman, and, still under the spell of the creature, would bring her to the place where she was to meet her horrible fate.

The creature would then rise up out of the dark hole and swallow the innocent young woman in a single bite, taking her down beneath the earth. The young man would be left dazed and would remember nothing of the encounter, but live the rest of his days with a terrible ache in his heart.

Well, a few hundred years ago, near the King's Inns, there lived a girl called Cathleen. She was sweet and kind, and had a quick mind.

Her father was also a kind man. He was a gardener at the Inns, just like his own father before him. It is said that all their family had a 'green finger' – that means people who are good with plants and gardening – but with this family, it also meant that they were favoured by the fairy folk. In fact sometimes members of the family were given magical gifts in return for tending the trees and flowers.

Before Cathleen's granddad died, he gave her a little leather pouch on a string.

'Now promise me,' he said, 'you'll always wear that around your neck. In your time of darkest trouble, it will be very useful to you.'

'Don't worry Granda,' said Cathleen, 'I promise, so I do.'

Now of course Cathleen was curious, and once or twice she dared to peek into the little pouch. Inside all she saw was what looked like a pile of seeds, nothing more. But she'd made a promise to her granddad, so she wore the pouch around her neck day in and day out.

One day, wasn't Cathleen out walking near the King's Inns when she passed by a man called Matthew standing there. Matthew was himself a fine young man studying at the Inns. The minute he saw Cathleen, his face lit up. He knew he had to get to know her better, so he approached her and started a conversation. I have to tell you, as soon as he came over, didn't her face light up too, and there was a great spark between them.

Each day, they would meet and walk together, talking about the ways of the world, their families and friends. Talking, in fact, about anything that came into their heads.

The important thing is that they were talking to each other.

Now this is all a lovely picture, but what of the darkness we spoke of earlier? Well, do you know what, things had been quiet and settled for many years – almost fifty years to the day in fact, since the dark hole rumbled. Now fifty years is a long enough time, and if people don't keep telling stories of what went before, it's easy enough to forget dark happenings of the past.

But you and I know about the tree that was felled. You and I know about the dark hole that was left, and you and I know too that fifty years had passed, and that meant the great hunger for revenge was coming again, and very soon!

This particular evening Matthew was walking in the grounds of the King's Inns, when he thought he heard a rumbling sound. Next thing he felt his head fill with a dark 'whoooooossssh', and his mind was emptied of all his thoughts.

The next day Cathleen was due to meet him for their usual walk. He was late. This was unusual, but she didn't think too much of it. Perhaps he was delayed in his studying?

After an hour or so, he finally arrived.

'I can't walk with you today, Cathleen,' he said, 'I have other things on my mind.' Matthew's face was pale as the moon, and his eyes had a strange look to them. It was as if they were made of ice.

'Are you ill, Matthew?' Cathleen said to him, with concern in her voice. 'Sure you're quite pale.'

But instead of answering her question he simply looked at her and said, 'You'll meet me at the bench near the gates of the Inns tonight at nine. Don't be late, it's important.'

And then he turned and left.

Now poor Cathleen didn't know what to make of that. She had never seen him be so cold with her. But she knew him to be a good man, so it must be something else that was on his mind.

She let herself feel a tiny flicker of happiness in her heart. 'Perhaps he wants to propose to me tonight? That's it! He is so pale and acting a little odd because he is so nervous!'

With this happy thought growing in her heart, off she went home, and about her day. When night fell she snuck out of the house (for her father wouldn't have been too happy about her going out so late), and made her way to where Matthew had asked her to meet him.

When she got there, sure enough, there he was sitting on the bench, waiting for her. He was looking straight ahead, not at her, but still she smiled at him. She turned her face to him and leaned in, expecting him to greet her with a kiss. But he didn't – he just kept staring ahead!

A cold wind whipped around the bench where they were sitting. Cathleen shivered, and drew her shawl tighter around her shoulders.

'What did you bring me here for, Matthew?' she asked him, growing a little worried.

Still he didn't answer.

'Matthew, are you listening to me?' she said, a little more insistently. Then she reached out and touched his arm.

At this, he shot up off the bench, as if he was disturbed from a deep sleep. A second later he slumped to the ground a few feet away from Cathleen.

'Matthew!' she cried.

Of course, her first thought was to jump up and help him, to see what was wrong, but when she tried to stand, she found that she couldn't move her legs – it was as if she was glued to the seat! The wind got suddenly colder around her, and her skin felt like ice.

'Help me!' she cried out, but it was dark, no one else was around, apart from Matthew who was lying stiff as a board on the ground.

A split second later she heard a horrible rumbling sound, and a huge black hole opened

up in the ground behind the bench. The black hole itself rose up into the air, and Cathleen heard the growling of a huge animal.

She turned her head to see hundreds of black teeth inside the hole. The creature was hungry and it was going to swallow her whole! This was the end of her for sure, and maybe Matthew too.

She closed her eyes tightly – then suddenly she heard a voice in her head. It was her granddad's voice. He was talking about the pouch he gave her. The one she always wore around her neck.

'In your time of darkest trouble, it will be useful to you ...'

Quick as a flash, she ripped the cord holding the pouch from her neck, and flung the whole thing backwards into the mouth of the dark hole. The pouch flew open and the seeds from inside were tossed high in the air. There was an almighty growl from inside, and Cathleen felt herself being pushed hard off of the bench and down on to the ground, right beside where Matthew was lying.

She turned to see the dark hole. It was huge and fierce; a big dark mouth of a creature, with flashing green eyes, and hundreds of long black teeth. It bit down into the bench where Cathleen had been sitting just moments before. But as it did, something incredible happened!

The colour of the dark hole began to change from black to brown; some of the long pointy teeth began to turn into what looked like branches, other teeth began grow back down into the earth, like huge roots, and the flashing green eyes began to change their shape into that of leaves.

Only moments seem to pass, and all that was left of the dark hole was a gentle rumble, and in its place was a huge and beautiful tree, one grown by the seeds from her pouch. Her granddad's present had protected her!

Cathleen turned to Matthew, who was just opening his eyes. The spell was broken, but he remembered nothing of the night, of course. He was very sorry that he had put his beloved into such danger, but of course it wasn't his fault, and she forgave him immediately.

She told him her other little secret, that she thought he was going to propose to her, and do you know what? Two weeks later he did, in that very spot (he needed two weeks to build up the nerve, but also to recover from their dangerous adventure)!

Now, you will remember that the dark hole creature was just about to eat Cathleen when it was turned into a tree. Well, what I didn't tell you yet, was that it was transformed into a tree mid-bite. That bench where she sat was trapped in its mouth!

So now to this very day, you can walk to the place where this all happened, and see where the dark hole was. You can see the beautiful tree it became. You can even see the bench that it swallowed, still trapped half in, half out of the trunk. Many call it the Hungry Tree, and say that it continues to eat the bench. We know what was there before was much more scary, though, and that changing it into a tree (with

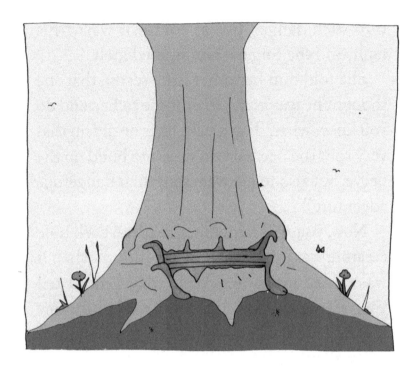

the help of some magical seeds) was a very good thing!

And do you know what, if you go there to see the tree, you just might bump into a great-great-great-great grandchild of Matthew and Cathleen, working there in the King's Inns as a gardener!

6

Mrs O'Flaherty's Chimney

Do you have a favourite teacher from school? Someone who you really like and enjoy learning stuff with? I have a couple I can remember even today. I think the reason they were my favourites is that they made learning stuff great fun! They were fair when talking to us kids, and they taught stuff in a way that was easy for us to understand.

This is a story about a teacher a bit like that. Her name was Mrs O'Flaherty, and she was a favourite teacher for many people in Dublin.

Mrs O'Flaherty always believed in finding fun ways to teach stuff. She believed in listening to what everyone had to say and always having good manners.

She was a great teacher, so she was!

Mrs O'Flaherty taught for many years in a school in the middle of Dublin. She'd often get thank-you cards and even presents from students she had taught years ago. Imagine that!

She must have made a good impression to be remembered even when they'd left school!

Mrs O'Flaherty had lived most of her life in the middle of Dublin City, because it was near to her job, but when she retired, she thought to herself, 'I think I would like to try living in a nice little place out in the country.'

Now Mrs O'Flaherty also lived with her black and white cat, Trouble. She loved him very much, and of course, she wanted to find somewhere that suited both herself and Trouble.

So, off she headed, in her little red car, to drive around and look for a new house for them to live in. Somewhere outside of the city a bit, where they could enjoy the fresh air, and maybe grow some flowers and vegetables in the garden. Trouble loved sniffing around vegetables!

Now it wasn't as easy as it sounds to find a new place. Mrs O' looked at some of the houses with 'For Sale' signs, and they were gorgeous, but many were too expensive for her to buy.

'You must be very rich to live in some of these places,' she thought.

She also found some houses that were in a nice place, but had been empty for ages and needed loads of work.

'That would be hard to do by myself,' she said, 'and I don't know how good you are with a hammer and nails and a drill, Trouble.'

Trouble gave a 'meowwww' (which in cat language meant 'not very good'). He was good at chasing mice, but not so good at fixing roofs at all.

Well, Mrs O' kept on looking at different places, and this went on for a few weeks. One week she drove over to visit a friend who lived near a place called 'The Strawberry Beds'.

Isn't 'The Strawberry Beds' a great name for a place? When I was small, I used to imagine that if you went there you'd find a load of little strawberries, tucked up in their blankets, snoring their juicy little heads off!

Now of course I realised later on that 'The Strawberry Beds' in fact got that name because a load of fruit was grown in the area back in 'the old days', and the ground where you grow strawberries is called a 'bed' (not the same as a bed with pillows). Still, I quite like the first idea too!

Back in the olden days, people used to take day trips over to The Strawberry Beds. It was such a lovely place, people would go over in horse and carts, and sometimes they'd take a picnic with them. There are a lot of old cottages over in The Strawberry Beds, even today.

Well, Mrs O' was driving in The Strawberry Beds this particular day, and she took a shortcut down a road she'd never taken before. There, on the side of the little road, didn't she spot a little cottage with a 'For Sale' sign near the gate!

Oh, it was the most beautiful little house she'd ever seen, and she fell in love with it on the spot. It had a thatched roof, white walls and red windows. It was lovely.

She thought for sure that she couldn't afford it, but she decided to ring the number on the 'For Sale' sign anyway. She was shocked when the man on the phone told her the price. She could afford to buy it!

The man selling the house (he was called the 'estate agent') told her that the old owner of the house had lived abroad for years, but had just had the house fixed up on his last visit. It needed a clean, and a lick of paint or two, but everything else was grand.

'When can I see it?' asked Mrs O' with excitement.

'Well, I just put the 'For Sale' sign up today,' he said. 'I'd say it's going to be very popular.'

'I'll take it!' said Mrs O'.

'What?' said the estate agent. 'But you haven't even seen the inside of it!'

'I don't care,' said Mrs O'. 'It's too lovely to let go. I want to come in to your office today and buy it!'

And do you know what? She did, without even seeing the inside! This was a very unusual thing to do when buying a house! She went home that night and told Trouble all about it.

'We have a new house!' she said.

Trouble looked up from his saucer of food and gave a 'mewww' (which in cat language is 'that's nice').

A couple of weeks later it was time for them to move house to The Strawberry Beds. A big van would follow them later in the afternoon with some of the extra furniture, but Mrs O' and Trouble would head over first thing that morning, with her car full of boxes, including everything needed to start cleaning and make a nice cup of tea!

They drove over from the city centre to The Strawberry Beds, then down a little road and in the driveway and up to the cottage. They parked the car, Mrs O' walked over to the house, and unlocked the door for the first time. The door creaked open. Creeeeeak.

Now inside, it was a bit dusty and had cobwebs in the corners, but apart from that,

it was exactly like she'd hoped it would be! There was even an old kitchen table and chairs that someone else had left behind, and an old-fashioned broom propped up against the wall.

'Let's get some of those boxes inside, Trouble, and then I can start sweeping,' she said.

Mrs O' started carrying in boxes, some cleaning supplies, her kettle, and some tea and milk and sugar. Now, you need a cup of tea when you are cleaning your lovely new cottage, so you do, and maybe a chocolate biscuit or two, and luckily she had brought a packet of those with her!

Chocolate digestives. Mmmm.

Trouble had no real interest in cleaning, so he decided to explore every nook and cranny of the cottage. This was going to be his new home, after all!

Off he went, sniffing out every corner, starting with under the table. Very nice. Then he headed over to investigate the fireplace.

Mrs O' picked up the old broom, and began to sweep the kitchen floor. Well, no sooner had she given the floor one or two licks of the broom, didn't a noise make her jump!

'MEEEEOOOOOOOOOOOOOOOOOOOOOOOOOOOOOOOOWWWWWWW!'

Trouble let out the biggest meow you have ever heard! He darted away from the chimney as fast as his little legs could carry him, and hid behind one of the packing boxes.

'Trouble! What are ya up ta at all?' said Mrs O'Flaherty, and she walked over to investigate whatever it was in the chimney that had frightened him.

But, as soon as she got there, didn't she let out a big noise, not far from a meow herself!

'OOOOOOOOOOHHHHHHHHHH!' she said, and backed away from the chimney, fanning her nose with her hand.

For down from inside that chimney came the worst smell Mrs O'Flaherty had ever smelled in her entire life! It was as if someone had made a big auld soup of mouldy cabbages, mixed with smelly socks, mixed that with bits of auld cheese and threw in a rotten egg or two to top it all off.

'Ooooh Lord have mercy!' said Mrs O'. 'That would melt the hairs outa anyone's nose! Trouble! Is that you? Do you need to go outside? Have you been a bould cat, have ya now?'

She looked over behind the boxes at Trouble, who was shaking his head very quickly.

'Don't blame me, Mrs O',' he thought. 'I did NOT make that smell!'

'Where is it coming from?' said Mrs O', and she looked around the room to see if perhaps there was some old food left rotting in a box, or maybe a wild animal had come in and left a surprise – but no. She saw nothing like that, and the smell did seem to be coming down from inside that chimney!

Well, next didn't she do the bravest thing, didn't she put her two fingers over her nose to stop the smell getting in, and didn't she stick her head inside the chimney! 'Let's take a look,' she said.

'My Missus O' is fierce brave,' thought Trouble.

No sooner had Mrs O' Flaherty done this, than didn't the loudest noise come down the chimney, and nearly knock Mrs O' to the floor.

'PHHHPARRRRRRRRRPPPPPPT!' went the noise.

Now, if you press your lips against your arm and blow, you can make a noise just like the one they heard (go on, give it a try so you get the idea ... ok? Done it?).

Well, the noise from the chimney was like that one, only MUCH, much louder! And, along with the noise came a big blast of air.

Now I say air, but what I really mean is a wind. And I say wind but what I really mean is a naaaaasty wind that smelled like that cabbagey-smelly-socky-cheesy-eggy soup!

Next thing isn't Mrs O' sitting in a heap on the hearth, with a bit of soot on her face, having been blown out of the chimney. She wasn't very happy! Trouble crouched down behind his box even more.

'Is there someone up my chimney?' said Mrs O' in a stern voice.

Silence.

'IS there someone up MY chimney?' said Mrs O' again, this time in her very stern voice! She held the old broom in her hands tightly.

Silence.

Then 'Phhhrarrrrrrpppht!' Another smaller blast of the stinky wind.

And then came a trembling voice from high up in the chimney.

'Y ... y ... yes.'

Now Mrs O' got a bit of a fright, as even though she was asking the question, she wasn't reeeeallly expecting an answer. Nevertheless, she kept calm, and spoke back to the voice.

'What's your name, then?' she said.

Silence.

'What is your NAME?' she said, and her voice was a little bit sterner. 'I have a broom in my hands, and I know how to use it if I have to!'

'Mmmm ... Michael,' said the voice. 'Mmmmm ... Michael Kelly.'

'Well now, "Michael Kelly",' said Mrs O', 'you'd better come down now from my chimney so you can talk to me.'

'Oh no, oh no, I can't, I can't,' said Michael, in a very frightened voice. 'I can never come down again!'

'Don't be silly!' said Mrs O'. 'Why not?'

Michael started to answer her. 'Because ... because I ...' then all of a sudden, 'PHHHPARRRRRRRPPPPPPT!'

It happened again, and a gust of stinky, stinky wind blew down on top of Mrs O', causing her to cough.

'See!' said Michael, in a very sad voice. 'That's why I can never come down.'

'Are you FARTING up my chimney?' said Mrs O', who was now annoyed as the stinky wind had blown more soot on her face and she had two white circles around where her glasses had kept the soot away.

She looked a little bit like a panda.

'Yes! Yes, I am farting,' said Michael, and all of a sudden didn't he start to cry, and his tears began to drip down the chimney too, also on top of Mrs O's head.

Now the more he boo-hooed the more he farted and so on and so on so it went like this: 'Boo-hoo PHHHPARRRRRRRRPPPPPPT sniff, boo-hoo PHHHPARRRRRRRRPPPPPPT sniff, boo-hoo PHHHPARRRRRRRR-PPPPPPT sniff.'

Now, Mrs O', as we've mentioned, was a very kind lady, and even though Michael was up her chimney, stinky and drippy and had covered her in soot, she felt sorry for him because he was so upset.

'Look, Michael, don't cry now. You come down here, sit at the table, and I'm sure we can sort all this out,' she said.

'PHHHPARRRRRRRRPPPPPPT sniff.'

'Are you sure?' said Michael. 'Are you really sure

you will be able for the smell? It's even stronger when I'm not in the chimney.'

'Yes, I'm sure! One moment, I'll get ready, then you can come down here, sit at the table and tell me your story,' she said. She looked around, and plucked a clothes peg from a basket and put it on her nose. 'All right, Michael. You can climb down now,' she said.

'Oh I don't need to climb anywhere,' said Michael. 'And there's one other thing I should probably tell you ...'

Mrs O' could hear Michael's voice getting louder. He was coming down the chimney.

'I'm a ghost,' he said.

The next thing didn't Michael Kelly pop right out of the chimney. And he was indeed a ghost! Mrs O' might have been a little bit frightened at seeing him, if it wasn't for the fact that she was distracted, as the first thing he did was 'PHHHPARRRRRRRPPPPPPT' and she had to cover her face as it was like a strong wind blowing her hair back.

'I'm very pleased to meet you,' said Michael. 'PHHHPARRRRRRRPPPPPPT.'

'Well, well,' she said. 'You really are a ghost. A farting ghost in the chimney of my new cottage! I never thought I would be saying those words! You'll sit down there at my table now, Michael Kelly, ghost or no ghost, and tell me all about why you are up my chimney.'

'I'll tell you my story,' he sniffed, 'but I can never sit at that table again.'

He began to sniffle again, sniff, sniff, while still farting away. 'PHAAARRRRRRPPPPP.'

And so Michael began telling his story ...

He told of how, a few hundred years ago, he'd been very friendly with the family who once lived in the cottage. The son had just come back from travelling and the family threw a big party to celebrate. They'd invited friends and neighbours over for a big dinner, and Michael was one of those people.

Now, also invited was a young woman called Mary. Michael really thought Mary was lovely and he was very excited that he would be able to talk to her a bit at this party.

Well, he arrived, and he was dressed in his good clothes, his shoes all shined, his tweed waistcoat, and his hair combed. He wanted to look his most handsome for Mary!

The guests were all seated at the table. Michael saw where his seat was to be and wasn't he delighted! His seat was set right next to Mary!

The night started off well; himself and Mary were chatting away, and the food, oh the food!

The table was covered with lots of delicious things, many of which the son of the house had brought back from his travels abroad. There were rich meat pies, sauces made with beans, beans covered in sauces, and vegetables that Michael had never even heard of, let alone tasted.

Everyone wanted to taste it all, and Michael was no exception. About a half an hour after the dinner had started, didn't Michael begin to feel a strange rumbling. At first, he thought he was hearing the rumble of a horse and cart passing by the window outside, vibrating the stone floor. The Strawberry Beds was a very popular place to visit from the town, and there were passenger carts that passed by all day long.

But then it slowly dawned on him. The sound was coming from his own tummy! He had been so busy talking to Mary, he hadn't realised how much he'd eaten. He'd been excited to try all the new foods, and serve some to Mary on her plate – 'Here, try this,' he'd say – that he had eaten way more food than he normally would.

Not only that, but some of the food on the table was food that he had never eaten a bite of before, and it was starting to do strange things in his tummy. The mixture of all the meats, and sweets and beans was brewing up a storm in there!

'Oh no,' he thought, 'I think there's a huge fart about to escape, what will I do?'

He was just about to get up from the table and go outside, when didn't the father of the house stand up to make a speech at the table. The 'Fear an Tí' clinked his fork on a glass and everyone fell silent.

'Dear guests,' he said, 'I beg your full attention for a little while, for what I have to say may be the most important words of my life ...'

Oh no. There was no way Michael could get up and leave the room in the middle of the speech. Important words. Everyone was listening. It would be so rude! What would Mary think of him? But, what of the alternative?

Rummmmmble rummmmmble. He could feel the gassy storm in his tummy grow bigger and bigger. There is no way he could let out that stormy fart in front of Mary! She was right beside him! And it would be so loud, it would interrupt the speech of the 'Fear an Tí'. He would try to hold it in, that's what he'd do. Maybe it would go away all by itself?

But no. The rummmmmmmble ruuuuummmble got louder and louder. Michael began to feel very unwell, and sweat began to pour from his head.

'Wait, hold on a minute!' said Mrs O'Flaherty, interrupting the story. 'You began to feel unwell? Surely then you got up from the table?'

'No, I didn't,' said Michael. 'But it got even worse. My tummy kept rumbling and rumbling and rumbling, and then the pain started.'

'Well, what happened?' said Mrs O', gripped by the story.

'I got sweatier and sweatier,' said Michael. 'In fact it was drip dripping off my head. The rumbling got louder and louder. I began to get dizzy. Rummmmmbbble rummmmble, drip drip it all went, rummmmble rummmmble drip, drip. Ouch. Even Mary was starting to notice. Rummmble, drip drip … She asked me if I was all right, but I couldn't answer. The pain was so bad now I had to close my eyes tightly like this.' Michael squeezed his eyes closed to show Mrs O'.

'Oh no! What happened next?' said Mrs O'.

Michael opened his eyes from squinting. He looked at Mrs O'Flaherty with his big sad ghost eyes and a tear trickled down his ghost cheek.

'I exploded!' said Michael. 'I exploded all over that table!'

And he gave out a big 'booo hooooo' and a 'PHAAAAAAARRRRRP!' at the same time.

'Oh dear. Oh you poor, poor thing, Michael,' said Mrs O' Flaherty. 'You exploded?'

'Yes,' he said. 'And I won't describe that for you any more. You can use your imagination. It was much worse than any fart could be. Poor Mary sitting beside me!'

He went on to tell Mrs O' how after his explosion, his ghost had then become trapped up the chimney, just like the big fart had been trapped in his tummy. He had been trapped up that chimney ever since that day. Most people could never hear him, but they could smell him. That's why people didn't stay very long in the cottage, even though it was otherwise lovely.

Mrs O'Flaherty went to give Michael a hug. Well of course, her arms went right through him, as he was a ghost, but he was happy that she had tried to anyway.

'Right,' she said. 'We are going to fix this. It's high time you got out and got some fresh air, and I can't be having farts coming down my new chimney all day.'

'But I'm trapped here,' said Michael. 'I can't go anywhere.'

'Yes you can,' said Mrs O'. 'Now, Michael, I want you to be brave. I want you to take a deep breath, and let out the biggest fart that you can. Right here. Sitting at the table.'

'Oh no!' said Michael. 'I really can't. It would be SO rude.'

'Just trust me,' said Mrs O'.

Well, Michael sat down at the table. He took a deep breath and out it came. 'PHAAAAAA AAAAAAAAAAAAAAAAAAAAAAAAAAAAA AAAAAAAAAAAAAAAAAAAAAAAAAAAAA AAAAAAAAAAAAAAAAAAAA ...'

The curtains began to blow in the wind.

'... AAAAAAAAAAAAAAAAAAAA-AAA ...'

Small boxes began to fall over.

'... AAAAAAAAAAAAAAAAAAAA ...'

The hair on Mrs O'Flaherty's head was blown back as if she was in a storm!

'... AAAAAAAAAAAAA ...'

She held on to the edge of the table with one hand, and held the clothes peg tighter with the other.

'... AAAAAAAAAAAAAAAAAAAAAAAA-AA-AAAAAAAAAAAAAAAAAAAAAAA-

AA-AAAAAAAAAAAAAAAAAAAAAA-
AAARRRRRRRRRRRRRRRRRRRPP-
PPPPPPPPPPPP!'

Mrs O'Flaherty tried to get to the window. But there was more!

'PHHAAAAARRRP. PHAAAAAAA-
AAAARP!'

Trouble peeped out to see if the coast was clear but –

'... PHAAAAAAAAAAAAAAAAAAA AAAAAAAAAAAAAAARRRRRRRRRP. PPPPP. PPP.'

Finally, after what seemed like ages, it was finished! The noise stopped, but the room was very smelly!

'Now, Michael,' Mrs O' said, 'I want you to repeat these words after me: "Excuse me."'

Slowly, Michael said the words. 'Excuuuuse me?'

There was a rush of air and Trouble began to peer his head out from behind the packing boxes.

'Now. How do you feel?' said Mrs O'.

'I ... I feel great!' said Michael. 'I feel like I just let go of a big worry.'

'That's because you did,' said Mrs O'. 'We all get gassy from time to time. Even me.' She giggled. 'But there's no point in holding it in if it's no good for you. You've been holding that worry in for the longest time, and now you've let it go. All it took was a little "excuse me" and it made it better. That's the great thing about good manners.'

She pulled back the old lace curtain, unlocked the window, and pushed it open. When she did, a warm gentle breeze blew in. This caused Michael to wobble a little bit, because remember, he was a ghost, and as thin as a wisp of smoke.

'Off you go,' she said to Michael.

'Really?' he said to her.

'Yes, really,' she said. 'You are long overdue some fresh air, and I have cleaning to do. Now off you go!'

'Goodbye, Mrs O'Flaherty,' said Michael. 'I can't thank you enough, so I can't.'

'Well now, Michael,' she replied, 'sure you just did thank me. Goodbye to you.'

With that, the ghost of Michael Kelly floated over the table and chairs, out the little window, and up into the blue skies until he could be seen no more. He did leave a smell behind him, but it wasn't the smell of stinky cabbagey-socky-cheesy-eggy farts.

Instead, it was the smell of all the wonderful foods and spices he had eaten that night before he exploded, all those years ago. The night he had sat beside Mary. The night she had held his hand and smiled at him. The night that had, for a while at least, been the happiest in his whole life.

The tall trees in the distance swayed in the breeze, and Mrs O' closed the window and sat down at her kitchen table.

She looked around at the cottage, her new home, and she was very happy. She was happy that during her first hours there, she had been able to help someone, which is something of course she still loved to do.

'What a pleasant ghost that was, eh Trouble? Are you hiding?'

Trouble peered his head out from inside an open box, and sniffed the air.

'No sign of Mr Stinkies any more,' he thought, and he climbed out of his box.

Mr Stinkies is the nickname he had decided on for Michael.

'I think you deserve a nice bowl of cream as a special treat,' said Mrs O'.

Now Trouble liked the sound of that!

Mrs O' picked out a blue saucer from one of the packing boxes, and a carton of cream from the shopping bag, and poured Trouble a bit of cream in the saucer beside the chimney.

Trouble didn't get cream very often, but it was one of his favourites, and he darted over to the saucer and began lapping it down at top speed.

'Go easy, Trouble!' said Mrs O'. 'If you drink it too fast you'll give yourself –'

But just as she was about to finish her words, out it came from Trouble: 'PHHHPAR-RRRRRRRPPPPPPT!'

He looked up at Mrs O' with an 'oops' face.

'I was about to say slow down, it will give you gas!' she laughed. 'Oh Trouble! Well, what do you say?'

Trouble looked up at Mrs O' and licked his lips. 'Mewww mewwww,' he said to her.

Which of course, in cat language is … 'excuse me'.

7

Dalkey Danny

Dublin Bay is a bay shaped just like a big letter 'C'. It stretches all the way around from Howth Head on one side, over to Dalkey Point on the other. Dotted along between those two points are many beaches and towns, and of course, in the middle is the entrance to the Port of Dublin City.

Over on the south side is Dalkey. There you will find Coilemore Harbour. In the olden days (and perhaps even today), if you went down to Coliemore Harbour, you would find the most interesting characters. Coliemore translates to *calach mór* in the Irish language. That means 'big harbour', which it is!

This place would often be full of people taking the sea air (very healthy!), walking their dogs, children playing, and, of course, the place would be full of fishermen at their boats.

One such fisherman was Danny. He was a big man with twinkling blue eyes, a face that had seen the sun a lot and a big scraggly dark beard. That could have described a number of the fishermen down at the harbour, however, you could usually tell Danny from the other lads with no problem at all.

The reason is that Danny was the only one walking around with a flower stuck in his hat! Now people would wear a flower in their jackets for a wedding or a special day sometimes, but a flower in the hat was quite unusual for a fisherman, particularly if you wore one every day.

Now, many people thought Danny was just being a little silly – maybe he was just an eccentric character – but if you took the time (which most people didn't!) to go over to Danny and talk to him, you would find out just why he wore a flower in his hat every day. In fact, you would, if you were interested enough, find out a lot of very interesting things from Danny.

His favourite thing to talk about above all was the weather. He knew loads of interesting stuff about the sea and the air, and if you asked him, he was happy enough to share his knowledge.

'Ah,' said he. 'A fisherman always needs to know the wind. Where it's coming from, where it's going, and most of all, where it might take me.'

Sometimes Danny would use the sand to explain the weather. He would take a stick and draw a circle within another circle.

'See that?' said Danny. 'Now, if you look out your window at night and you see the moon, with a big circle around it, well, you know that it's bound to be a wet and stormy day when you wake up in the mornin'!'

If a bird landed down beside him he would sing a little rhyme to it, 'Seagull, seagull, sittin' on the sand, sure 'tis never good weather when you stay on land.'

'Ah, all of the animals know more than we do about the weather,' Danny would tell you.

If you had a cat, he would tell you to watch her near the fire place.

'If she sits with her back to the fire, or if she even tries to go in to the empty grate, well then you might very well have some bad weather on your doorstep soon.'

If you had a dog, he would tell you to listen out for the way it speaks.

'Now a dog ...' said Danny, 'a dog loves telling you things. All you have to do is listen. If your dog makes a certain type of howl or odd noises, he could be telling you that a storm is coming ... or if you have a pig even better!'

He'd say, 'If you see a pig walking through Dalkey collecting sticks, then you know for sure there's a bad winter coming.'

You might pause for a moment and think: 'How in the world would a pig pick up sticks with its trotters?' (I know *I* had that thought!)

When Danny was asked that question, he would say nothing but simply chomp his teeth together in a biting motion: 'CHOMP CHOMP'. Aha. Just like a dog would carry a stick. In its mouth (but maybe you guessed that already!).

Now we've had a fair few bad winters since then, but I have yet to see a pig walking through Dalkey gathering sticks. But maybe they did it when I was asleep, because Danny seemed right about most of the other things.

When he was off fishing, there was no talking to him. He was a man on a mission. A mission for fish!

He liked to fish on his own, 'To have a bit of time to meself,' he'd say. When he landed his catch he would tell you a bit more about the fishing, how it was.

He'd tell you of the different types of fish to be caught: pollock ('them fellas love hiding in the rocks'), mackerel ('sure on a good day, they do be hopping out of the water at ya!'), plaice ('with spots like a leopard!') and wrasse ('stocky lads. They're fond of a crab for breakfast').

He would tell you great stories of big and strange fish caught over the years in Dalkey. His voice got particularly quiet when he would tell you the story of a certain Willie Flanagan's catch …

'It started plain enough. Willie, Ned, Pat and Mick set off for the normal fishin'. They had mixed luck with the catch, although Ned was having the worst night of them, poor fella. First he caught a big pile of nothin', next didn't his net get snagged and tangle and then finally, when he thought he had a bite, didn't he catch a poor seagull and had to release it with great squawking (mostly Ned's)!

'It was coming on for nightfall, when didn't the lads feel a great tug on the net. They looked overboard and there it was – face like a demon – a huge conger eel!'

Danny's eyes got wider! 'Though, you know what, it might as well have been a sea monster, the size of it!

'Well, that eel knew it was in trouble, and took off in a flash, so it did. Diving and squirming and twisting – and so began the tug of war between the men and the monster!'

Danny was standing up now, using his hands and arms to tell the story. One arm was the

boat, the other the sea monster. It was like a strange dance, twisting and turning like a stormy sea.

'The boat was being pulled this way and that by the huge thing, and every so often you'd hear a cheer from the crowd who had gathered on the beach to watch them!

'Finally, didn't Ned grab tongs from the floor of the boat, and SNATCH the eel out of the water! PLOP! It went on the floor of the boat – well most of it, some of it was still in the water! As it squirmed and tossed, the men stood well back – sure the boat was tossing to and fro!'

Danny was in full dance now, arms waving, legs hopping from one to the other.

'Up went the boat, down went the boat, and in the middle of all this sure didn't they lose one of the oars. Luckily, Ned had his wits about him, and he used the tongs and his hands to row one side back to shore.'

Back on shore of course, there was great celebration and a huge crowd gathered around the men.

'When the eel was landed, the measuring tape was sent for. It was a great sight, the four lads standing beside it. And wait 'til I tell ya, wasn't it NINETEEN AND A HALF FOOT LONG! Well, even Ned could say that was a good night for fishing after all!'

Now, while Dalkey Danny always went fishing on his own, if the day was fine and he met some tourists that he thought were nice people, he would take them out for a spin in the boat. He wasn't a tour guide himself, but sure he may as well have been. If there was an interesting fact to be told, Danny was the one to tell it.

Out on the waves he would point over to Killiney Hill. He would tell the visitors about the 'Druid's Chair'. Now the Druids were a high-ranking bunch of people years ago. They were teachers, poets, priests and even judges. Many people looked to the Druids for wisdom and advice, and some people even thought them to be quite magical. The chair is made from slabs of very big stone and is in the middle of a wood.

'Now,' said Danny, with his serious face on, 'if you wanted a judgement on something, or a dispute settled, you would go before the Druid sitting in the chair, and hope you were not going to get into trouble.'

If the tourists looked very serious during this story, Danny would crack a smile or wink at them. But if they weren't taking his story seriously enough, he would get even more serious-looking himself!

You can still see that Druid's Chair up in Killiney today. It's sometimes called 'The Judgment Seat'.

When he had tourists from Holland visiting, Danny was quick to point out, 'Sure we had our own windmills too! We had one right up there in the quarry.'

Indeed it was true, there had been a windmill there, but what he didn't tell the tourists is that it didn't work very well and only lasted about fifteen years.

If the tourists were lucky, Danny would dock his boat at Dalkey Island and give them a 'tour'. What a great spot.

He would tell you about St Begnet, the 'Patron Saint' of Dalkey; there's a church named after her on the island.

'She was an Irish princess, so she was. Many say she came from down the road.' Danny would point over his shoulder and down the coast. 'She always wore a bracelet, and people say it was given to her by an angel!'

He would point out the wildlife: the seals, the black rabbits, the herd of wild goats, the

terns and all the other birds that love to visit
there too.

'Sure they all love to visit here,' Danny would
laugh. 'Birds, saints, and even the Vikings!'

While Dalkey Island is only five minutes
from the harbour in the boat, Danny could

make it the trip of a lifetime. He could talk for hours and still have his audience at the edge of their boat benches listening!

But wait a minute. Did I never tell you why Danny wore a flower in hat? Sure that was what started me off in the first place!

Well, of course, it all comes back to Danny's favourite subject. Do you remember? Yes. The weather.

Danny would tell you the time of when he was a young lad himself, and his grandfather would teach him how to read the wind with grass and flowers. He would show Danny how you could throw a bunch of petals or the stems of grass in the air, and watch how they blew away – that would tell you both the direction and the strength of the wind.

'Daisy petals are best!' Danny would say. 'Better than any weathervane or machine! Now you won't find many daisies growing out there on the waves. That's why I always like to keep one tucked inside my hat, for good measure! I have my machines and the smell of the air to guide me, but still, there's nothing like throwing up a good bunch of daisy petals, just like when I was a lad!'

And that's the story of why Dalkey Danny used to wear a flower in his hat.

So, you see, if things seem a little strange or unusual in the world, there's often a very good and interesting explanation behind them, if you just take the time to ask and listen!

8

Filou Filou

Did you know that over the years, many different groups of people from around the world have come and made Dublin their home? These people have always been drawn to our shores for at least a thousand different reasons. With so many different experiences, there must be so many different stories.

Some people came who were warriors, and wanted to raid the land. Others came as explorers, and landed here, sometimes by accident. Some people came to be reunited with family. There were also people who came to escape hard times in their own countries, and make a brand new start in Dublin. One such group of people was called the Huguenots.

The Huguenots originally came from France, but in their home country at the time, many people disagreed with the their religion and politics. Because of this, most of the Huguenots left their home to find somewhere to live that was safer. A large number of them came to Ireland, and many settled in the capital city of Dublin.

Jack was a young Huguenot man who had come over to Ireland on a ship when he was small. His uncle had travelled with him, but had settled in a different part of the country and Jack was left to fend for himself. Jack was a bright young man with a big heart, and was happy to learn a trade and work hard, so soon he took the job of tailor's apprentice in Dublin. His boss, Mr Millet the tailor, was a very different type of man altogether – and not a very nice one! He was very selfish.

As an apprentice to Mr Millet the tailor, Jack worked long hours, slept in the corner of a cold workshop, and was given very little to eat. Mr Millet knew that Jack was unlikely to complain, as he was all alone in a new city and this work was better than no work at all. Jack did most of the hard work, yet Mr Millet took all the credit!

However, despite this hard life, Jack learned to sew quickly, and, as the months went by, it was clear that he had a great talent for sewing. In fact, he was on his way to becoming a much better craftsman than his own boss Mr Millet!

Jack was particularly good at the kind of sewing that needed fine detail, like embroidering flowers, making lace, or the fine stitching of a delicate shirt. Mr Millet of course let Jack do all this fine work, but claimed credit for it himself whenever a compliment was passed by a customer.

Jack often found himself sitting in the cold workshop, working long into the night, sewing all the delicate pieces that his boss had left for him to finish.

One night, having worked for ages, and having had very little food, Jack began to fall asleep at the work table. His eyes were just

about to close, when he heard a noise. At first he thought it must have been a mouse, as it was a kind of scratching sound, coming from underneath the work table.

But when Jack bent down to investigate, it not a mouse that he found. There, underneath the table, was a tiny man. In fact it was a fairy man! He was dressed all in green, and was wearing a cap with a feather in it. His little leg had become trapped in the crack between the floorboards, and he was trying, in vain, to escape.

Under the little man's arm was tucked a tiny morsel of bread. It was just a crumb to us humans, but for the fairy man it was the size of a good big loaf.

Jack reached in to help the little man, but the fairy's eyes flashed like flame, and he hissed back.

'It's all right, little man, I won't hurt you,' said Jack.

The little man stopped hissing, but gave a scowl.

Jack reached in, and just managed to free the little man's leg. No sooner had he done so, than quick as a flash, didn't the little man shoot off into the darkness. Jack looked down and saw the little man's coat, caught on a splinter. He had slipped out of it to escape. Beside the coat was the little crumb-loaf of bread. The little man must have dropped that too while escaping.

Jack picked up the little coat. It was one of the most beautiful pieces of clothing that he had ever seen! It was the colour of moss in the middle of a forest. The sewing work was so fine, and it was made with a type of silk like none Jack had ever seen. So soft! However, when it caught on the splinter it had also torn. Jack decided to try to repair it.

He took the coat over to his mending table, and picked out the tiniest needle he could find. He looked for a spool of silk to match the colour. There was no thread slender enough to fit his needle, so he carefully unwound a small piece of silk, and divided it into strands, until there was one thin enough to fit through the eye of the needle.

Very carefully, with a squinty eye, he threaded the needle and began to sew. It was very slow work, as he had to be so careful with each stitch in the delicate fairy fabric.

Finally, once he had mended the tear in the little man's jacket, he carefully laid it out on the floor, just beside where he had first encountered him. Then Jack remembered the crumb-loaf, and the fact that the little man seemed hungry. Jack placed the crumb-loaf beside the coat, and beside that he also added a little crumb of cheese. Jack had little food himself, but a tiny crumb of cheese would be a feast to a little fairy man.

Jack knew he still had his regular work to do, and went into the other room to fetch more mending. When he returned, just a few minutes later, he found that the jacket and the bread and the cheese were already gone! In their place was a large spool of the finest silken thread he had ever seen. He picked it up to examine it.

It was not a single colour, but seemed to be made from the skin of a rainbow. When Jack held it to a blue cloth, it became the colour of the sky; when he held it to a green cloth, it became the colour of the forest, and so on and so on. It was a match to everything. What a fine gift the fairy man had given him! He would save it for a very special garment.

Jack sat down to do his work, and yet again his eyelids began to droop from tiredness. He could hear a song in the distance, yet there was

no one in the workshop with him. In fact the song seemed to be coming from inside his own head:

'Filou filou fil-ay-ree-oh, a fairy-oh, now off you go. Filou filou fil-ay-ree-oh, with silk I sew, fil-ay-ree-oh.'

Now this song was very beautiful. It also seemed strangely familiar to Jack. He recognised two words as being from his old language – French. 'Filou' meant 'trickster' and 'fil' meant 'thread'. Hmmm. What did this mean?

The more he heard the song, the sleepier he became, and it wasn't long before he drifted off, with his head on his arms there at the work table.

SMACK! Jack awoke suddenly when he felt a hand whack him on the back of his head.

'I don't pay you to sleep, boy!' roared Mr Millet. 'And what's this?' he said, picking up the spool of fairy thread.

'It's … it's …' Jack couldn't find the words to answer his employer, and he probably wouldn't have believed his story of the fairy man anyway.

'It's mine! That's what it is,' laughed Mr Millet cruelly. 'You work for me, so it's mine now.'

Mr Millet took Jack's fairy thread over to his own work table, and started to do the regular mending with it. 'It's mine now,' he muttered to himself.

That evening it was Jack's job to deliver the day's mending. On top of his job as an apprentice, he was also a delivery boy, a cleaner, and whatever other job Mr Millet made him do.

In the delivery pile was a pair of grey trousers to go to a rich businessman, a red dress to deliver to a posh lady; and there was a brand new white shirt to take to the lord mayor's house.

'Be careful with those clothes, boy,' said Mr Millet, 'particularly with the mayor's shirt.'

Now, Jack himself had made the mayor's shirt, he had spent hours on it. Of course he would be careful. He delivered all the mending and clothes and came home to a cold workshop again, exhausted and hungry.

The next day, some strange things started to happen around the city of Dublin. The businessman had just turned a corner. He kicked a cup from the hands of a couple of beggars on the side of the road. He laughed and continued walking down the road, near

St Stephen's Green, when didn't he hear someone singing a little song:

'Filou filou fil-ay-ree-oh, a fairy-oh so off they go. Filou filou fil-ay-ree-oh, with silk I sew, fil-ay-ree-oh.'

There was no one singing that he could see. Well, next thing didn't his grey trousers fall off! They literally came apart at the seams and fell to the ground. The businessman was standing there with the breeze blowing around his bottom!

Now the businessman wasn't too far from his house, but still he had to run half naked down the road to get there. He passed the beggars who he had been mean to earlier. They had a good laugh and pointed at him.

'The state of yer man! Could you not afford trousers, sir? Will we loan ya a few bob, sir?'

Now if you'd been there, and you'd looked very closely, you might just have glimpsed a tiny man watching all this from behind a railing. He was wearing a green jacket, had a twinkle in his eye, and was holding a length of fairy thread in his hand.

'Filou filou fil-ay-ree-oh, a fairy-oh so off they go!'

The businessman was very angry when he got home. He would have words with the tailor in the morning.

Over on the other side of town, the posh lady was holding a tea party for her friends. She had just scolded her poor maid for being a 'slow servant' and had made the girl cry. The posh lady was just reaching for a sandwich, when she thought she heard a little voice singing:

'Filou filou fil-ay-ree-oh, a fairy-oh so off they go. Filou filou fil-ay-ree-oh, with silk I sew, fil-ay-ree-oh.'

Of course she couldn't see anyone at all, and had no idea where the voice was coming from. But wait 'til I tell ya – next thing wasn't the lady standing there in her undergarments!

Her red dress had fallen off and was lying there on the ground. Her lady companions tried not to giggle, but couldn't help themselves, and it cheered the poor maid up no end. Now if you'd been there, and you'd looked very closely, you might just have glimpsed a tiny man watching all this from behind a curtain. He was wearing a green jacket, had a twinkle in his eye, and was holding a length of fairy thread in his hand.

'Filou filou fil-ay-ree-oh, a fairy-oh so off they go ...'

The posh lady had never been so embarrassed in all her life. She would march over to that tailor first thing in the morning.

In fact, all over Dublin other people who had gone to this particular tailor were losing their clothes. Garments were falling to the ground without explanation. It was as if a thief had stolen the thread right from the seams of their clothes! And each time it happened, a strange little song was heard, yet nobody was to be seen.

The funny thing about it was that it didn't happen to everyone – the losing of clothes – only to those who added a mean streak to their day.

In one house in particular, things were different. In one house, no clothes fell off at all. This one house was the house of the lord mayor of Dublin.

The lord mayor was a powerful man, but he was also known for his warmth and kindness. That evening he was getting dressed for an official dinner. He was putting on his shirt when he noticed a detail on the collar. It was a tiny flower, sewed perfectly by Jack. It reminded him of when he was a boy growing up in the countryside, and of his family that he loved. He smiled, and walked out to his dinner, happy and confident. As he descended the stairs, he heard a faint song trailing on the landing behind him. He looked behind him but there was no one there.

'Filou filou fil-ay-ree-oh, a fairy-oh now off you go ...'

Now, if you'd been there, and you looked very closely, you might just have glimpsed a tiny man watching him from the bannisters, with a green jacket and a twinkle in his eye. This time there was no length of fairy thread in his hand. Instead he just stood there smiling.

The next day when the tailor opened his shop to the public, there was a queue of angry people waiting outside. All their clothes had fallen off the day before. They were demanding their money back, and threatening the tailor that they would never come back to his shop again.

The tailor was very confused. He had mended their clothes himself, and he had done it quite well. He had to think quickly, to save his own skin.

'My dear customers,' he said. 'I am so very sorry. I must apologise on behalf of my apprentice Jack. I am a generous man, and I believed him ready for the task of sewing your clothes, but sadly I was wrong. He has been lazy in his work with your garments. I assure you he will be punished for this!'

The customers grumbled, but were a little less angry when they believed their clothing mishaps to be the fault of a young lazy boy.

When the last of the customers had left, Mr Millet turned to Jack.

'No food for you tonight, boy! For I did promise my customers I would punish you,' he said, laughing at his own lie.

'But Mr Millet, I –' Jack was just about to protest his punishment, when the door swung open.

It was the lord mayor of Dublin himself. He was holding a white shirt in his hands, and had a serious look on his face.

'Oh no,' thought Mr Millet.

For it was one thing for the gentry of Dublin to be annoyed with Mr Millet and his shop, but a whole other thing for the lord mayor of Dublin to be upset with him.

'His clothes must have fallen off him, too,' thought Mr Millet. 'I must do something!'

'Your worship! You are most welcome to my humble shop. And before you say another word let me tell you that it was this lad!' said Mr Millet, pointing at Jack. 'This lad that sewed your shirt and caused you injury. I know, I know, common punishment is not good enough for him! I shall throw him out on to the street this very night for offending you.'

The lord mayor turned to Jack, a little confused. 'Boy,' he said. 'Did you sew this shirt?'

Jack looked at the collar. It was indeed his work this time.

'Yes, your worship,' said Jack, bowing his head. 'I was the one who sewed your shirt.'

The lord mayor gave a big smile. 'Well, what wonderful work it is,' said the mayor. 'You are a talented young man. I came here to reward your employer for his talent, but I see now that I was mistaken. You lad, you are the talent.'

Mr Millet's face dropped! He was sure the mayor was there to give out, not give praise!

'Emmm, I believe I was mistaken, your honour. It was I who sewed your shirt. The boy merely fetched me the thread.'

The lord mayor's face grew angry. 'Sir. There is nothing I like less than liars in my city. It is obvious to me now that you are both a cruel man AND a liar. In light of the fact you are about to throw the boy out on to the street, let me now offer him employment.'

The lord mayor turned to Jack. 'Come with me, lad. You will make a fine tailor. In fact someday you may even become the head tailor of Dublin City!'

Jack couldn't believe his luck! He walked to the door, and as they were leaving the lord mayor turned around to Mr Millet.

'And you! Be thankful that I don't have you arrested! You will be lucky from this day forth to be asked to sew sacks of potatoes, never mind clothing!'

The door slammed, and Mr Millet was left standing there, alone in his empty tailor's shop.

Jack went to work for the lord mayor, and from that day on his life was so much better! He had a beautiful workshop to work in, a warm bed to sleep in, and as much food as he needed to fill his belly.

He continued to make the most beautiful of embroidery pieces. People remarked on the quality of the work, and of course the thread – he had the most unusual thread! It was as if it was made from the skin of a rainbow! When you held it to a blue cloth, it became the colour of the sky, when you held it to a green cloth, it became the colour of the forest, and so on and so on. It was a match to everything. Although many asked him where he got it from, Jack never told his secret. Perhaps you can guess?

Every night, when Jack had finished his work, he would go to his dinner table, and set an extra place for a guest. He would place a tiny plate (made from a metal button), a tiny mug (made from a thimble), and a tiny knife and fork (made from sewing needles and pins).

He'd light a candle, and wait for his guest to arrive. Have you guessed who the guest was? His guest was his old friend the tiny fairy man, still wearing his (mended) moss green jacket and a cap with a feather in it. The two of them would sit and talk about their day. If there was any fairy mending, the little man would leave it for Jack to fix.

Fairies were famous for mending everything in the world, the little man told Jack once, so it was so very nice to have someone else do it for them once in a while. And Jack was happy to help.

The little fairy man would always leave a gift for his friend. Spools and spools of fairy thread, as much as you could ever use in a lifetime.

This was the thread that seemed to be made from the skin of a rainbow. When you held it to a blue cloth, it became the colour of the sky, when you held it to a green cloth, it became the colour of the forest, and so on and so on. It was a match to everything.

This was thread that was as strong as an ox, but that could just as easily melt away into air at the soft command of the right song.

Years passed and young Jack did indeed become the head tailor of Dublin City and lived a long and happy life.

To this day, if you are walking up around Merrion Square in Dublin, you might still hear a certain little song in the air, and no one to be seen singing it.

Now if you have brought a mean streak to your day, hold on to your trousers, for you soon may find them in a heap on the ground! But if you have been kind in your day, the fairies themselves might appear at your feet to give you a blessing:

'Filou filou fil-ay-ree-oh, a fairy-oh, and off we go. Filou filou fil-ay-ree-oh, with silk I sew, fil-ay-ree-ooooooooooh ...'

9

G'wan Oura Dat

When I was growing up in Dublin, one of the best places to hear stories was when you'd be out playing with your pals on the street. Sometimes a story was made to rhyme, and kids would use it when they were playing a skipping or clapping game.

Sometimes kids would play a game called 'Knick Knock', which was knocking on people's doors with a 'rat-a-tat-tat', running away, and hiding. Now this is all well and good if you like jumping up to answer the door all the time, but not as much fun if you've just put on your slippers and are relaxing by the fireplace with a cup of hot cocoa and your favourite book!

There was one game I remember playing called 'German Jumps'. Now this was a game where you knotted LOADS of elastic bands together into a big long circle. Then two people stood as the 'posts', holding the elastics apart like a big long rectangle. When it was your turn, you had to jump over and between the elastics. It started easy, when the elastics were around the ankles ('anklies'), but got harder as the elastics were moved higher ('kneesies' etc.) and made very narrow (one-leg jumps). As you were jumping, everyone else would sing a rhyming story.

German Jumps had a few different names. I've also heard it called 'Elastics'. When I got older, I heard it called 'French Skipping', 'Airplane', 'Japanese Jumping' and 'England/ Ireland/Scotland/Wales'.

Isn't that funny, all those names for the same game? My friend who studies history and knows loads of other important things said there is a very old game from China that is a bit like it, and that it might have started with that game. Imagine that. This is such an old game that kept being passed on, and kept changing its name.

That game is a bit like stories; passed on for years, with little bits changing every time a new pile of people try it out.

Here I have a rhyming story for you. Of course, you don't have to jump when you are saying it (but you can if you like)! Some of these rhyming stories have actions (things you might make up and mime along with the story), like saluting every time someone says 'queen or king', or tipping an imaginary hat when the rhyme says so. You can make these actions part of the game too, and of course you can try making up your own versions.

If you read it out loud, you can play around with the rhythm of the words, so they fit your jumping. You might have to stretch some words out to make them longer and say some other ones quite quickly to make them fit!

This old man lived up our street,
The grumpiest fellah you ever would meet.
When you knocked at his door with a
 rat-a-tat-tat,
Sure he'd roar out the window: 'G'wan
 Oura Dat!'

He ate fried sausages for his tea,
And he wouldn't give any to you and me.
If your ball went over, that was that,
You'd never get it back from G'wan Oura
 Dat.

He had a yellow budgie called Kidney Pie,
Now she was the apple of his eye.
But one day Kidney Pie flew out,
Got stuck in me Nana's chimbley spout.

We clapped our hands and gave her a
 fright,
An' up she flew into the night.
We caught-her-in-me-cousin Johnny's
 jacket,
She made an awful squalkin' racket.

So down we went to G'wan Oura Dat,
And we banged on his door with a
    rat-a-tat-tat.
'What's all this?' said G'wan Oura Dat.
'With yiz bangin' on me door with the
    rat-a-tat-tat?'

Now under me arm was a bird so
    black,
Pee-pin' out from an auld coal sack.
Covered in soot from a chimbley pot,
And happy as Larry that she was
    caught.

'Oh Kidney Pie, you've come back home,
You didn't leave me all alone!'
We saw an aul' tear come to his eye,
And back in the house flew Kidney Pie!

He thanked us all, said we were great,
And he gave us sausages from his plate.
'That's your reward for stopping by,
And rescuing my Kidney Pie.'

'How do youse do, my name is Pat,
No more I'll say, "G'wan oura dat".
Now youse are all me nicest friends,
I'll find a way to make amends.'

Next thing over his back wall,
Came thirty-seven lost footballs.

'There yiz go,' said the old man Pat,
An' he closed the door, and that was that.

Now years they come and years they go,
And some jump high and some jump low.
But I'm never too old to tip me hat,
To the man we called 'G'wan Oura Dat'.

10

Sugary Tea

Peter O'Reilly was very fond of a good cup of tea. He'd particularly look forward to one when he came home from his job. He worked as a porter for the ships down on the North Wall Docks.

His wife Mary could tell how hard a day he'd had by the number of sugars he asked for in his tea. On an easy day, he'd only have the one, but if it was a long day, or he came home stressed out, he would ask for more. Two, would be a long day, and the very odd time, even three. But this particular day, in walked Peter and asked Mary could he have five sugars in his tea!

'Five? Did you say five?'

Of course Mary knew something must have happened, so she got him his sugary tea, sat him down and told him to tell her all about his day at work.

Peter's day had started out normal enough. He was a bit tired starting off but nothing unusual, as he hadn't had a great sleep the night before. He knew, though, that his day would get much busier. In a couple of hours there was a ship called the *Slieve Bawn* coming in to dock. It had sailed from Liverpool, and when it arrived in the port all the cargo would need to be unloaded and inspected.

The ship came in on time as expected, and many workers helped unload all the cargo. It was Peter's job to walk around the cargo crates, and make sure nothing got broken while it was being unloaded.

He was walking by this big wooden crate, when he heard a sound.

'Tap. Tap. Tap. Tap.'

At first he thought he imagined it (he was a bit tired after all).

'Tap. Tap. Tap. Tap.'

He heard it again! Maybe it was a piece of wood knocking in the wind? But there was no wind!

'Tap. Tap. Tap. Tap.'

It was definitely coming from the crate. Peter was a little bit afraid, but he knew he had to investigate. That was his job, to make sure everything was all right. So off he ran, got a crowbar (a tool for opening things), and began to crack open the wood on the side of the crate.

Well, when he opened up the crate, didn't he get the shock of his life! Inside the crate, there was an upside-down man!

At first glance Peter thought he was looking at some kind of a white statue inside.

'Help,' said the statue.

Peter jumped back for a second in fright, then realised it wasn't a statue, but in fact a live human being!

After inspecting a bit further, Peter saw that this was a man who was covered head to toe in white plaster. Head to toe, except for a few

air holes and his face and hands. That's how he managed to tap on the side of the crate with his fingers, 'tap tap tap tapping' on the wood.

Peter shouted for help, and when his workmates came, they very carefully lifted the man (who was upside down, remember?) out of the crate. They called for an ambulance and carted the man off to Jervis Street hospital, because they had to see if he was all right. They also needed to cut all the white plaster stuff off him.

The plaster was the same kind you'd have on a cast if you broke your arm, except this man had it all over his body. Just like with a cast, it is put on wet and wound around you like a bandage, and when it dries, it is rock hard, like stone. So, any part of you encased inside it couldn't move at all!

Later that day, Peter found out from his boss why the man had been in the crate in the first place.

The upside-down man was named Maurice de Laboujac. He was a French painter who lived in London. His paintings were to be shown in an Art Exhibition in Dublin, but he wasn't able to get official visitor papers to come to Ireland himself. He still really wanted to come, though, and to get around the problem of no papers, he came up with the idea of 'posting' himself to Dublin, disguised as a statue in a crate.

He had a friend cover his whole body in white plaster so he wouldn't get bruised and hurt when the ship was moving about at sea. He spent four whole days in that plaster while the crate was on its journey.

His plan was going fine until the ship docked in Dublin. Didn't some of the ship workers unload the big wooden crate upside down! Poor Maurice was inside, and of course, if you're upside down all the blood can flow to your head and make you dizzy. Maurice couldn't move because he was trapped in the plaster, so it was then he realised that he needed help! So he began to 'tap tap tap tap' with his free hand. He kept on tapping until eventually Peter found him.

Apparently, Maurice was a little shook up, Peter's boss said, but he was grand once they cut the plaster off him in the hospital.

'That's a very stressful day you had,' said Mary, when she'd heard the story. 'Are you all right, Peter?'

'Ah, I got a bit of a fright,' said Peter, 'but it's nothin' that a sugary cup of tea can't fix.'

'No wonder you asked for five sugars,' said Mary. 'But do you know what? I betcha yer man Maurice the Frenchman needed about ten!'